The Emperor's
New Clothes

Many years ago, there lived an emperor who adored fashionable clothing and dressing stylishly. He spent all his money on clothes made of the finest fabrics and most sophisticated designs.

He didn't care for royal responsibilities and took no interest in governing or in his soldiers. In fact, the emperor never went out in public unless it was to make an appearance to show off the latest addition to his ever-expanding wardrobe.

The emperor had an outfit for every hour of the day should he choose to change that often.

He loved donning his clothes and admiring himself in the full-length mirror of his royal dressing chamber. There was even a saying amongst his people that "the emperor is in his dressing room," instead of sitting in council.

The city that the emperor lived in was very large, and many visitors came and went all the time. One day, two swindlers arrived, claiming to be magnificent weavers.

The so-called weavers declared that they could weave cloth into the most beautiful designs. But it was their most unusual claim to fame that caught the emperor's attention: the clothes made from their fabrics had the remarkable ability of being invisible to anyone simpleminded or who was not suited to their job.

This is incredible! thought the emperor. *If I wore such clothing, I'd be able to see which of my officials aren't doing their jobs properly, and it would be easy to spot who is simpleminded.*

"I must get myself some of these clothes made!" cried the emperor, and with that, he generously paid the swindlers more than the high price they demanded to ensure that his clothes would be the best they had ever made.

The swindlers swiftly assembled their looms and pretended to set to work straight away. It all looked very professional, minus one obvious detail: there was nothing on their looms!

The so-called weavers demanded the finest silk and strongest thread, and it was given to them at once. They snuck the luxurious materials into their own bags, and continued their imaginary weaving.

The emperor was quite pleased with himself for hiring the so-called weavers, and was anxious to see what progress they had made. Although confident in himself and doubtful of the likelihood, he was still nagged by the possibility that he would visit the weavers and not see anything on the looms. He decided to send one of his most hardworking, trustworthy officials to monitor the progress in his place.

Meanwhile, the news of the magical clothing had spread throughout the city, and everyone was now intrigued by the possibility of discovering the uselessness or stupidity of their neighbors.

The official sent to visit the swindlers knew, as everyone did, about the magical cloth. When he arrived at the workshop, he saw firsthand the swindlers toiling with great effort on empty looms.

The official was about to blurt out that there was nothing there, when he stopped himself.

Is it possible that I'm simpleminded? he silently panicked. *It can't be true! I must pretend otherwise, or I'll be out of my prestigious job!*

The swindlers noticed the official pause, and one of them said:

"Well, what do you think? Isn't it beautiful?"

The official cleared his throat, and despite the obviously empty loom, gushed:

"Yes, yes of course! It's wonderful! Absolutely exquisite! Such fine craftsmanship!"

The swindlers acted quite pleased with themselves, and continued laboring away. They made quite a good show of cutting invisible thread with their scissors, and readjusting the invisible cloth that in fact wasn't there at all.

Upset that he was not as smart as he thought he was, the official reported back to the emperor that the weavers in the workshop were making wonderful progress, and that his new clothes would be ready sometime soon.

The emperor was thrilled with the news, but he was not a patient man. A few days later, he was again curious to know what progress had been made since the last visit. He took the opportunity to send along a different official to see if this man was also competent.

Meanwhile, the swindlers demanded more silk, more money, and more gold thread. As the first official's report had been glowing, the emperor agreed to each request. Once again, the swindlers pocketed the high-quality materials.

Soon, the second official paid the crafty weavers a visit. It was the same story as with the first minister. The second official came to the same conclusion, and out of fear of losing his job, exclaimed that the lovely design was the most exquisite he'd ever seen.

By now, the emperor was quite satisfied with the two reports. He decided that it was time to visit the weavers himself. Accompanied by the two ministers who had visited before him, he arrived to check on the progress.

"Your Majesty, isn't this the finest design you have ever seen?" gushed the two officials.

The emperor stood before the looms in silent horror, for he saw nothing there. But there was no way that he was going to make this confession! He praised the swindlers for their hard work and superb design, and agreed to wear the new clothes in the upcoming grand parade.

The day of the parade, the emperor stripped down to his underwear. When he was dressed, although it was plain to see that in fact he wasn't, the emperor's attendants oohed and aahed:

"A perfect fit! Such delicate cloth!"

The emperor looked at himself in the mirror and pretended that he was pleased with his fine new outfit.

A chamberlain bent down and pretended to pick up the emperor's train. He held out his hands as though he was in fact holding something, and didn't dare to pretend otherwise.

The emperor marched along in the parade and everyone watching pretended that these new clothes were his finest yet. No one dared admit that they couldn't see his new outfit. That would mean that they weren't smart or that they were unfit for their jobs!

Suddenly, the voice of a small child rang out:

"But he isn't wearing anything!"

It wasn't long before the child's remark spread throughout the crowd.

"It's true! He isn't wearing anything at all!" everyone shouted at last.

The emperor cringed. He was beginning to think that it was true–that everyone was right! He decided that there was nothing left to do but continue along. Followed by the chamberlain, who carried his train that really wasn't there at all, the emperor held his head high and proudly marched down the street.

Meanwhile, somewhere on the outskirts of the city, two swindlers carried heavy loads but smiled nonetheless. They were never seen again.